STATE TREES

★ ━━━━━━━━ ★

including the Commonwealth of Puerto Rico

Also by Sue R. Brandt

FACTS ABOUT THE 50 STATES
HOW TO WRITE A REPORT
STATE FLAGS
including the Commonwealth of Puerto Rico

STATE
TREES

INCLUDING THE COMMONWEALTH OF PUERTO RICO

★  ★

BY SUE R. BRANDT

FRANKLIN WATTS
NEW YORK ★ CHICAGO★ LONDON ★ TORONTO ★ SYDNEY

★ ▬▬▬▬ ★

For my children,
Yvonne Mary and Derek Joseph

The author expresses special thanks to the secretaries of state, state foresters, and other officials in the fifty states who generously and most graciously supplied information on which the content of this book is based.

The poster referred to in the introduction was published by the National Association of State Foresters under an agreement with the U.S. Forest Service of the U.S. Department of Agriculture.

Photographs copyright ©: Arizona Office of Tourism: p. 11; Comstock Photography: p. 15 (Art Gingert); Visuals Unlimited: pp. 37 right, 59 (both John D. Cunningham), 17 (Arthur R. Hill), 40 (Valorie S. Hodgson); Linda Boyes/ Hawaii Visitors Bureau: p. 20; Texas Department of Tourism: p. 52. All other photographs copyright © Donald J. Leopold.

Library of Congress Cataloging-in-Publication Data

Brandt, Sue R.
State trees / by Sue R. Brandt.
p.   cm.
Includes bibliographical references and index.
Summary: Describes each state's official tree and how it was chosen.
ISBN 0-531-20000-0 (lib. bdg.) — ISBN 0-531-15632-X (pbk.)

1. State trees—United States—Juvenile literature.   [1. State trees.   2. Trees.   3. Emblems, State.]   I. Title.   II. Series.
QK85.B73   1992
582.16′0973—dc20   92-8946   CIP   AC

CONTENTS

★ ▬▬▬▬▬ ★

INTRODUCTION   7
ALABAMA   Longleaf Pine   9
ALASKA   Sitka Spruce   10
ARIZONA   Paloverde   11
ARKANSAS   Shortleaf Pine   12
CALIFORNIA   Coast Redwood, Sierra Redwood   13
COLORADO   Blue Spruce   14
COMMONWEALTH OF PUERTO RICO   Ceiba   15
CONNECTICUT   White Oak   16
DELAWARE   American Holly   17
FLORIDA   Cabbage Palmetto   18
GEORGIA   Live Oak   19
HAWAII   Kukui   20
IDAHO   Western White Pine   21
ILLINOIS   White Oak   22
INDIANA   Tulip Tree   23
IOWA   Oak   24
KANSAS   Eastern Cottonwood   25
KENTUCKY   Kentucky Coffee Tree   26
LOUISIANA   Bald Cypress   27
MAINE   Eastern White Pine   28
MARYLAND   White Oak   29
MASSACHUSETTS   American Elm   30
MICHIGAN   Eastern White Pine   31
MINNESOTA   Red Pine   32
MISSISSIPPI   Southern Magnolia   33
MISSOURI   Flowering Dogwood   34
MONTANA   Ponderosa Pine   35
NEBRASKA   Eastern Cottonwood   36
NEVADA   Single-leaf Pinyon, Bristlecone Pine   37
NEW HAMPSHIRE   White Birch   38
NEW JERSEY   Northern Red Oak   39
NEW MEXICO   Pinyon   40

NEW YORK   Sugar Maple   41
NORTH CAROLINA   Longleaf Pine   42
NORTH DAKOTA   American Elm   43
OHIO   Ohio Buckeye   44
OKLAHOMA   Eastern Redbud   45
OREGON   Douglas Fir   46
PENNSYLVANIA   Eastern Hemlock   47
RHODE ISLAND   Red Maple   48
SOUTH CAROLINA   Cabbage Palmetto   49
SOUTH DAKOTA   Black Hills Spruce   50
TENNESSEE   Tulip Tree   51
TEXAS   Pecan   52
UTAH   Blue Spruce   53
VERMONT   Sugar Maple   54
VIRGINIA   Flowering Dogwood   55
WASHINGTON   Western Hemlock   56
WEST VIRGINIA   Sugar Maple   57
WISCONSIN   Sugar Maple   58
WYOMING   Plains Cottonwood   59
STATE ARBOR DAYS   60
FOR FURTHER READING   61
INDEX   62

INTRODUCTION

★ ━━━━━━━━━━━━━━━━━━━ ★

During Earth Day celebrations in 1990, many people received posters showing all the state trees. At the top the poster said, "Be Careful with Our Stately Treasures." Most people said they had never before seen all the state trees together in one large beautiful picture. Smokey the Bear was at the bottom of the poster with oak leaves and acorns in his hatband. He was there to warn us to be careful with fires when we go camping in the woods or forests.

Earth Day is a time when all of us—young and old—think about what we need to do to make the earth beautiful and healthful. We especially think about trees, and we go out and plant them.

Long before we had Earth Day, we had another special day for planting trees—Arbor Day. It began in Nebraska in 1872. Nebraska is one of the states that in early times had lots of tall grass but few trees. Settlers who went there to live wanted trees. To get them, they had to plant them, and that is how Arbor Day began. At first Arbor Day occurred on the same date in April in all the states. But April is not the best time in every state for planting trees. Now each state has its own Arbor Day. (There is a list of all the state Arbor Days at the end of this book.)

As the poster reminds us, trees and forests are part of our country's natural treasures. Over 800 kinds of trees are native to the United States. There are many environments in our country, and many kinds of trees adapted to them. Some trees and environments are common, some are rare.

In choosing a tree, each state thought about all the kinds of trees that grow naturally within its borders. The tree it chose was the one it thought best represented the state and its people for one reason or another. Some of the states asked school-children to choose the tree by vote.

A tree does not become a state tree just because people say it is. After a tree is chosen, the legislature (the lawmaking body) of the state must pass a law saying that it is the state tree. When the law is passed, we say that the state has adopted that tree.

Although there are fifty states, there are only thirty-eight different state trees because some states have adopted the same tree. The sugar maple, for example, has been adopted by four states. Do you know your state tree when you see it?

Note: In this book the state trees are described state by state, and the states are arranged in alphabetical order. Two names are given for every tree. The first is its common name, the one most people use to identify the tree. The second name, the one in brackets, is the name scientists use.

ALABAMA

Longleaf Pine [*Pinus palustris*]

The longleaf pine belongs to the pine family. This big family includes the different kinds of pine, spruce, hemlock, and fir trees. They are called conifers—trees that have cones and leaves that are shaped either like needles or like scales.

The longleaf pine gets its name from its needles, which are often more than 10 inches (25 cm) long. They grow in bundles of usually three to a bundle. After several years they drop off, and new needles take their place. The long cones are made up of scales that are tipped with spines, or prickles. Older trees are straight and tall—from 75 to 120 feet (23 to 37 m).

Alabama chose the longleaf pine in 1949 because it is a valuable tree. It provides lumber for building, wood for making paper, and resin, which is used to make tar and turpentine.

The longleaf pine is also *North Carolina*'s state tree; see page 42.

ALASKA

★ ■■■■■■■ ★

Sitka Spruce [*Picea sitchensis*]

The Sitka spruce was in the wings of the *Spirit of St. Louis*, the plane that carried Charles A. Lindbergh on his historic flight across the Atlantic Ocean in 1927. In those days, airplanes were made of spruce, cloth, and plywood. Builders of planes used the Sitka spruce partly because its wood has unusual strength for its weight. The close-grained wood is also highly valued for musical instruments. The Sitka spruce is the largest spruce in North America and perhaps in the world. Older trees are usually 150 to 200 feet (46 to 61 m) tall, and some live to be more than 400 years old. Sitka spruces have sharp-tipped green needles that stand out all around the branches. The long cones ripen in a year.

In 1962 Alaska chose this tree because it is beautiful, it bears the name of the historic town of Sitka, and its wood is of very great value.

ARIZONA

★ ▬▬▬▬▬ ★

Paloverde [*Cercidium floridum; Cercidium microphyllum*]

In the spring, the paloverde (or palo verde) tree lights up the desert with its bright yellow flowers. This unusual tree belongs to the legume (pea) family, and its Spanish name means "green stick." Soon after its leaves come out in the spring, they drop off. In this way, the tree saves moisture that it otherwise would lose through evaporation in the dry desert air. The leaves are made up of pairs of leaflets on a branched leafstalk. The small flowers develop into pods that ripen and scatter their seeds in midsummer. Two kinds of paloverde trees are native to Arizona—the blue paloverde and the yellow paloverde. Both are small trees with wide-spreading branches and many spiny, or thorny, twigs. The blue paloverde has bluish-gray bark and somewhat flattened seedpods. The yellow paloverde has yellow-green to gray bark and rounded pods that are constricted (pinched in) between the seeds. It grows at lower elevations and in drier areas and is the smaller and more common of the two. Both kinds were adopted as the state tree in 1954 because the paloverde is one of the most unusual and most beautiful trees of Arizona's deserts.

▬▬▬▬▬

ARKANSAS

Shortleaf Pine [*Pinus echinata*]

Like the longleaf pine, the shortleaf pine is named for the length of its needles, usually about 4 inches (10 cm) long. The short cones are about half as long as the needles, and they grow on very short stalks. They ripen in two years but often stay longer on the branches. Older trees may be more than 100 feet (30 m) tall. Their reddish-brown bark is broken into scaly plates shaped like rectangles.

Arkansas adopted "the pine" as its state tree in 1939. But information from the state says that "the shortleaf or yellow pine" is the tree that was meant. Its lumber is used for building and for making furniture, doors, and boxes.

CALIFORNIA

★ ━━━━━━━ ★

Coast Redwood [*Sequoia sempervirens*]
Sierra Redwood [*Sequoia-dendron giganteum*]

California has the tallest and biggest trees in the country and the world. The coast redwood is the tallest, and the Sierra redwood the biggest. California adopted both trees, under the name "California redwood," as the state tree in 1937. They grow only in California, except for some coast redwoods in Oregon.

The tallest coast redwood is about 367 feet (112 m) high, and many others reach 300 feet (91 m). The tallest of these evergreen trees are probably over 2,000 years old. The cones have many tiny seeds, but few of the seeds grow. New trees come mainly from sprouts on the stumps of cut or fallen trees.

The Sierra redwood is often called the giant sequoia or big tree. The biggest one of all is 275 feet (84 m) tall and about 30 feet (9 m) across the trunk. It is estimated to be 3,500 years old. On older trees, the bark may be as thick as 2 feet (0.6 m). The leaves are small scales that grow in layers around the twigs. The cones have very small winged seeds, and these giant trees grow from the seeds. The stumps do not sprout.

Coast Redwood

Giant Sequoia

COLORADO

★ ▬▬▬▬▬▬ ★

Blue Spruce (or Colorado blue spruce) [*Picea pungens*]

The blue spruce decorates mountain slopes in Colorado, Utah, and other Rocky Mountain states. Young trees look like small Christmas trees. Older trees may have the same shape, but they are 60 to 100 feet (18 to 30 m) tall. The needles are short and four-sided with sharp points at the ends. They grow all around the branches and give the branches a bristly look. The cones ripen in a year. The name "blue spruce" comes from a bluish, waxy coating on the needles of some trees. If the needles do not have this coating, they are green. Colorado chose this tree, under the name "Colorado blue spruce," as its unofficial tree in 1939.

Utah has adopted the same tree; see page 53.

COMMONWEALTH OF PUERTO RICO

Ceiba [*Ceiba pentandra*]

The ceiba (SAY' buh), also called the silk-cotton or kapok tree, is a giant tropical tree. The seedpods contain a fiber usually called kapok. Because it is soft, fluffy, and almost waterproof, kapok became well known as a stuffing for cushions, sleeping bags, and life preservers. Today foam rubber and synthetic fibers take the place of kapok for many uses.

Many ceiba trees are over 100 feet (30 m) tall. Their huge trunks have buttresses (thick ridges) that extend downward and often spread far out around the trees. Each leafstalk has several leaflets about 5 inches (13 cm) long. New leaves usually appear each year, but the trees bloom every other year. "Ceiba" comes from the Caribbean Indian name for a canoe. Long ago dugouts (boats) were made from the trunks of the trees.

The Institute of Culture of Puerto Rico has proposed the ceiba as the official tree, but it has not yet been adopted.

Pathfinder
School

CONNECTICUT

★ ━━━━━━━━━ ★

White Oak [*Quercus alba*]

Native Americans knew the white oak tree well. They taught the early colonists how to boil its sweet acorns for use as food. White oaks may be 100 feet (30 m) tall or more and wider than they are tall. The leaves are divided into sections called lobes. The lobes are rounded and smooth along the edges. In autumn the leaves turn reddish brown. People admire the white oak for its strength and beauty. They like to use its wood, especially for floors and furniture. Its acorns feed many different kinds of wildlife. Oak trees are members of the beech family.

In 1947, Connecticut chose the white oak because one special white oak tree has stood for love of freedom in Connecticut since colonial days. In 1662, the English king granted the colonists a charter that gave them an unusual amount of freedom. The next English king sent his agents to Hartford in 1687 to take the charter away from them. But the colonists found a way to save it. They hid it in the hollow trunk of a white oak, which became known as the Charter Oak.

The white oak is also the state tree of *Illinois*, page 22, and *Maryland*, page 29.

DELAWARE

American Holly [*Ilex opaca*]

Almost everyone recognizes holly boughs with their prickly green leaves and bright-red berries. People are so fond of holly as a Christmas decoration that the American holly no longer grows in some places where it once was plentiful. It is a pyramid-shaped evergreen—50 feet (15 m) tall or more—with many short, slender branches. The leaves stay on the tree for about three years and then drop off in the spring. The small white flowers are either staminate (male) or pistillate (female). They grow on separate trees, so that only trees with pistillate flowers have berries. The tree is a member of the holly family.

Delaware adopted the American holly, one of its most important forest trees, as the state tree in 1939.

FLORIDA

★ ━━━━━ ★

Cabbage Palmetto (cabbage palm) [*Sabal palmetto*]

The cabbage palmetto grows straight up from a single, large bud at the top of the trunk. People sometimes use this bud, or cabbage, as a vegetable, but removing the bud may kill the tree. The cabbage palmetto reaches its greatest height—50 to 80 feet (15 to 24 m)—in Florida. Its huge, shiny, dark green leaves are shaped like fans. They are 5 to 8 feet (1.5 to 2.4 m) long and are divided into many long, drooping strips. In the spring, clusters of tiny greenish flowers appear among the leaves. By autumn, they ripen into smooth, rounded fruits. Each fruit has a single seed. On young trees the dead leafstalks cling to the trunks and make a crisscross pattern around them. Older trees are ringed with scars where the old leaves have fallen off.

The cabbage palmetto has many uses, especially in Florida, which adopted it as the state tree in 1953. The palm strips that are given to people in church on Palm Sunday come from its leaves. The leaves are also used to make baskets, hats, and other articles. The trunks are used as piles for wharves, and fibers from the leafstalks and bark make good brushes and brooms.

The cabbage palmetto is also the state tree of *South Carolina*, page 49.

━━━━━

GEORGIA

Live Oak [*Quercus virginiana*]

No one who sees live oaks ever forgets them. Gray "beards" of Spanish moss often hang from their huge branches. The moss does not hurt the tree, but it sometimes hides the thick, oval-shaped leaves. The live oak gets its name from the leaves, which remain green until new leaves come out in the spring. Many live oaks are 50 feet (15 m) tall and two or three times as broad. It is said that American Indians used the acorns to make a kind of flour to thicken their venison stew. The wood has been used in many ways, especially for shipbuilding in early times. In 1937, Georgia adopted the live oak because it had long been a favorite tree in the state.

HAWAII

Kukui (or candlenut) [*Aleurites moluccana*]

The kukui, or candlenut, tree has the lightest-colored leaves of all Hawaiian trees. They are light green with a powdery surface. The candlenut tree is a relative of the tung tree, which is known around the world for tung oil, made from its oily nuts. The candlenut tree also has oily nuts. Long ago the oil was burned to provide light in stone lamps or other candlelike devices. Some candlenut trees have twisted trunks and low-growing branches. Others are straight and 80 feet (24 m) tall with no branches near the ground. Their small, greenish-white flowers are often used in leis (Hawaiian necklaces). Leis made of the nuts are highly prized. Hawaii adopted the candlenut tree in 1959 because of its many uses in ancient Hawaii and its value to Hawaiians of today.

IDAHO

Western White Pine [*Pinus monticola*]

The western white pine resembles the eastern white pine, the state tree of Maine and Michigan. Both have needles that grow in bundles of five and cones that have no prickles. But the western white pine is taller. Its needles are shorter, and they grow more thickly on the branches. Its cones—usually about 8 inches (20 cm) long—are larger. The tree may live for several hundred years and grow to heights of 100 to 175 feet (30 to 53 m). The grayish-purple to reddish bark of mature trees is broken into smooth blocks. Idaho adopted the western white pine in 1935. It has more of these fine lumber trees than any other state, and the manufacture of lumber and other wood products is one of Idaho's most important industries.

ILLINOIS

White Oak [*Quercus alba*]

The schoolchildren of Illinois chose the white oak as the state tree. It was adopted in 1973. From 1908 to 1973 the state tree had been "the native oak," meaning any oak that grew in the state. The white oak is described under *Connecticut*, page 16.

INDIANA

Tulip Tree (or yellow poplar) [*Liriodendron tulipifera*]

People always notice the flowers and leaves of the tulip tree. The tulip-shaped flowers have six greenish-yellow petals, tinged with orange, that form a deep cup. Below the cup there are three creamy sepals (leaflike structures). The wide, lobed leaves have a shape that often looks like the outline of a tulip. The flowers develop into dry, cone-shaped fruits with many seeds. Forest-grown tulip trees may be 150 feet (46 m) tall, but trees that grow in the open are much shorter. The tulip tree has long been called a poplar tree, perhaps because its leaves seem to dance in the breeze, as poplar leaves do. Its wood is sold as "yellow poplar," but it is not a poplar. It belongs to the magnolia family.

Indiana adopted the tulip tree as the state tree in 1931. It was called the monarch (ruler) of the great forests that covered much of Indiana in pioneer times.

The tulip tree is also *Tennessee*'s state tree; see page 51.

IOWA

Oak [*Quercus*]

Iowa chose "the oak," meaning all the kinds of oaks that grow in the state, as its state tree in 1961. Several reasons were given. Almost all the woodlands in the state have at least one kind of oak, and most have several. No other group of trees seems as important to people and wildlife. Many animals and birds depend on the acorns of oak trees for food and on the trees for shelter and nesting places. Two kinds of oaks described in this book may be found in Iowa. One is the white oak, the state tree of *Connecticut, Illinois,* and *Maryland.* The other is the northern red oak, the state tree of *New Jersey.*

KANSAS

★ ▬▬▬▬▬ ★

Eastern Cottonwood [*Populus deltoides*]

The name "cottonwood" comes from the bunches of silky white threads on the seeds of cottonwood trees. When the seedpods open, the tiny seeds fly away on their cottony wings. The small seedpods hang from the twigs in strings 6 to 8 inches (15 to 20 cm) long. They grow only on trees that have pistillate flowers. Staminate flowers are on separate trees.

The cottonwood's shiny green leaves are shaped like triangles. They have toothed edges and pointed tips. The long leafstalks are flattened in such a way that the leaves rustle in the slightest breeze. The trees are usually medium-sized. Cottonwoods are poplar trees, members of the willow family.

Kansas adopted the eastern cottonwood as its state tree in 1937. It grows naturally along rivers and streams in Kansas. Pioneers planted it on their treeless homesteads, and it is still being planted in many parts of the state.

The eastern cottonwood is also the state tree of *Nebraska*, page 36. The plains cottonwood, page 59, is *Wyoming*'s state tree.

▬▬▬▬▬

KENTUCKY

★ ▬▬▬▬▬▬ ★

Kentucky Coffee Tree [*Gymnocladus dioica*]

It is not hard to guess how the Kentucky coffee tree got its name. Early settlers used its seeds as a substitute for coffee. The seedpods grow only on trees that have pistillate flowers. Staminate flowers are on separate trees. Each pod has several seeds separated by a mass of pulp. The pulp sometimes was used for soap in early times.

The leaves of the Kentucky coffee tree are huge—from 1 to 3 feet (0.3 to 0.9 m) long. They are divided into sections, and each section has a number of leaflets. But the tree has no leaves for about half of the year because they come out late and drop off early. Coffee trees are medium-sized to tall, with short, stubby branches. The tree is a member of the legume (pea) family.

Kentucky adopted the Kentucky coffee tree in 1976 because the people think of it as their own special tree. Before the Kentucky coffee tree was adopted, the tulip tree had been the unofficial state tree.

LOUISIANA

★ ━━━━━━ ★

Bald Cypress [*Taxodium distichum*]

Bald cypresses are trees with knees. These trees often grow in swamps and along rivers. In these places, the roots send up solid cone-shaped structures, called knees, that stick up above the water or muck. It was thought that the knees help supply oxygen to the roots, but careful investigation has failed to detect any such activity. Besides having knees, the tree is unusual in other ways. Its trunk tapers from a swollen, fluted (grooved) base. It is a conifer, a member of the redwood family, but it sheds its needles each year. They grow along the sides of small branchlets. In the autumn, the branchlets fall off along with the leaves. The cones ripen in one season. Bald cypress trees usually are from 65 to 130 feet (20 to 40 m) tall.

Louisiana adopted this tree in 1963. Its wood is said to last forever, and the wood has had many different uses in Louisiana from earliest times.

27

MAINE

Eastern White Pine [*Pinus strobus*]

The tall, straight trunks of New England's white pines were just right for use as masts of sailing ships in colonial times. All trees with trunks big enough for this purpose were declared to be the property of the English king. This action made the colonists angry and caused a great deal of trouble just before the Revolutionary War. It is thought that the early trees were twice as tall as the eastern white pine of today, which is from 75 to 100 feet (23 to 30 m) tall. But it is still the tallest conifer in the northeast, and it is still prized for its wood as well as its beauty. The needles grow in bundles of five. The slender cones—usually about 5 inches (13 cm) long—are slightly curved, and their scales have no prickles.

Maine adopted the eastern white pine as its state tree in 1945. Maine took its nickname, the Pine Tree State, from this tree. The tree's cone and tassel is the state flower, and the tree appears on the state seal and the state flag.

The eastern white pine is also the state tree of *Michigan*, page 31.

MARYLAND

White Oak [*Quercus alba*]

Maryland adopted the white oak as its state tree in 1941. One special tree, named the Wye Oak, stands for all the white oaks in Maryland. The state owns this tree and protects it in Wye Oak State Park at Wye Mills. It is more than 400 years old and over 100 feet (30 m) tall, and its branches spread out for a distance of about 160 feet (49 m).

The white oak tree is described under *Connecticut*, page 16.

MASSACHUSETTS

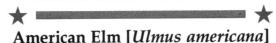

American Elm [*Ulmus americana*]

The American elm is a beautiful shade tree. Often it is shaped like a vase or a fountain. Before the leaves come out in the spring, the tree is covered with clusters of purplish flowers. These soon develop into clusters of oval-shaped fruits. Each fruit has a single flat seed. The leaves are oval-shaped and lopsided at the base, and they have toothed edges. The usual height of elm trees is 75 to 100 feet (23 to 30 m). In recent years a fungus called Dutch elm disease, spread by a bark beetle, has killed many elm trees all over the country.

Massachusetts adopted the American elm in 1941 in memory of the first Liberty Tree, an elm tree that stood in Boston in colonial times. Groups of people in the colonies met under special trees called Liberty Trees and talked about ways of gaining freedom from England. In 1775, English soldiers cut down the Liberty Tree in Boston and chopped it into firewood.

The American elm is also the state tree of *North Dakota*, page 43.

MICHIGAN

Eastern White Pine [*Pinus strobus*]

Michigan adopted the eastern white pine as its state tree in 1955. This tree played an important part in the growth of lumbering, one of the state's earliest and greatest industries. People in northern Michigan still tell many stories about lumberjacks who worked in the forests in times gone by. The tree is described under *Maine*, page 28.

MINNESOTA

★ ▬▬▬▬▬▬ ★

Red Pine [*Pinus resinosa*]

The red pine is often called the Norway pine, but no one knows why. It is thought that Norwegian lumberjacks of early times gave it the name because they mistook it for a pine that grows in Norway. The name "red pine" suits this tree well. It has a flaky, brownish-red bark, and its wood is light red. The green needles grow in bundles of two. The cones are small, and their scales have no prickles. Some trees are more than 100 feet (30 m) tall and have no branches for two-thirds of their height.

Minnesota had a number of reasons for adopting the red pine in 1953. For one thing, it grows naturally there and can be seen in many parts of the state. For another, it supplied much of the timber harvested in Minnesota in years gone by and added to the state's wealth.

MISSISSIPPI

★ ▬▬▬▬▬▬ ★

Southern Magnolia [*Magnolia grandiflora*]

Mississippi schoolchildren chose the southern magnolia as the state tree by vote, and it became the official tree in 1938. The tree often looks like a pyramid of glossy, dark green leaves with no trunk or branches in sight. It is always green because it sheds old leaves as new ones come out in the spring. The leaves of the southern magnolia are shaped like long ovals with pointed tips. The blossom is Mississippi's state flower. It is a beautiful flower—large, white, and waxy. The flowers develop into cone-shaped clusters of seedpods. When the pods are ripe, each one sends out one or more coral-red seeds that dangle for a while from slender threads. Southern magnolia trees vary in size and shape according to where they grow.

MISSOURI

★ ▬▬▬▬▬ ★

Flowering Dogwood [*Cornus florida*]

When the flowering dogwood tree is in bloom, it is a mass of white flowers—or what seem to be flowers. Actually, the four white "petals" are not the petals of flowers. They are bracts (leaflike structures) that grow around the true flowers. These are tiny greenish-white blossoms at the center of the bracts. The tree is usually small, sometimes 10 feet (3 m) but sometimes quite a bit taller. When autumn comes, the oval-shaped leaves turn scarlet, and clusters of bright red fruit hang from the tips of the branches. Each fruit has one or two seeds. Nurseries sometimes sell specially developed trees with pink or red bracts.

Missouri chose the flowering dogwood, one of its most beautiful trees, as the state tree in 1955. It is also the state tree of *Virginia*, page 55.

▬▬▬▬▬

MONTANA

★ ▬▬▬▬▬ ★

Ponderosa Pine [*Pinus ponderosa*]

The name "ponderosa" means ponderous, or of very great weight. It is a good name for a tree that may be as tall as 200 feet (61 m), have a trunk 8 feet (2.4 m) across, and may live as long as 500 years. The needles grow in bundles of three or sometimes two on the same tree. The large cones have scales with sharp prickles. A tree only 100 years old has dark-colored bark. On older trees the bark turns to a bright reddish orange. It breaks up into scaly plates that often look like the pieces of a jigsaw puzzle. Montana adopted the ponderosa in 1949 because it is beautiful and it has been a valuable timber tree from pioneer times to the present.

NEBRASKA

Eastern Cottonwood [*Populus deltoides*]

Nebraska adopted the American elm as its state tree in 1937. But the Dutch elm disease killed many elm trees, and Nebraska decided in 1972 to adopt the sturdy cottonwood. It has been an important tree in Nebraska since early times. Pioneers traveling westward in wagon trains along the Platte River looked for groves of cottonwoods as places to rest and meet other travelers. Early settlers planted cottonwoods on their homesteads, and today they grow throughout the state. The tree is described under *Kansas*, page 25.

NEVADA

Single-leaf Pinyon (or single-leaf piñon) [*Pinus monophylla*]
Bristlecone Pine [*Pinus aristata*]

Nevada has two state trees—the single-leaf pinyon and the bristlecone pine.

The single-leaf pinyon (or piñon) is the only pine tree with needles that grow singly rather than in bundles. The cones have large seeds, or nuts, that are good to eat. The tree is small, usually about 20 feet (6 m) tall. In 1953, Nevada adopted this tree because its nuts once were an important food, and its wood was used as fuel in Nevada's early mining industry.

Bristlecone pines are believed to be the world's oldest living trees. The very oldest tree of this kind yet found is about 4,600 years old. It happens to be in California. The trees are from 20 to 60 feet (6 to 18 m) tall. Many are twisted and worn-looking, and the oldest ones are almost bare of branches and bark. Nevada adopted the bristlecone pine in 1987 because it is proud of having several groves of these unusual trees.

Bristlecone Pine

Single-leaf Pinyon

NEW HAMPSHIRE

★ ━━━━━━━━━ ★

White Birch (or paper birch) [*Betula papyrifera*]

Native Americans used the bark of the white birch tree to make canoes and coverings for tepees. The bark can also be used as a kind of writing paper. It is white, tinged with yellow, and it separates into long, narrow, horizontal strips. The oval-shaped leaves have toothed edges and pointed tips. The fruit clusters look like little cones. They develop from small pistillate flowers that are pollinated by the drooping tassels of staminate flowers on the same tree. When they are ripe, the tiny winged nutlets fly away on the wind. Some white birch trees are as tall as 80 feet (24 m). The New Hampshire Federation of Garden Clubs suggested the white birch as the state tree, and it was adopted in 1947. It is an important part of New Hampshire's beautiful scenery.

NEW JERSEY

★ ▬▬▬▬▬▬ ★

Northern Red Oak (or red oak) [*Quercus rubra*]

The color red shows up in the new leaves of the red oak. They are reddish pink. The leafstalks keep a reddish tinge when the leaves turn dark green in summer. The autumn color of the leaves is a rich maroon. The bark of the tree is dark brown to black, but the wood is reddish brown. The leaves are divided into seven or more pointed lobes with bristle-tipped teeth along the edges. Because the acorns have a bitter taste, squirrels do not scurry to gather them as they do the sweet acorns of the white oak. Red oaks are usually 60 to 90 feet (18 to 27 m) tall, but some are much taller. New Jersey adopted the red oak in 1950. It is a favorite shade tree for homes, streets, and parks, and its wood has many uses.

NEW MEXICO

★ ▬▬▬▬▬▬▬ ★

Pinyon (or piñon, or nut pine) [*Pinus edulis*]

New Mexico's state tree has seeds, or nuts, that are good to eat. One of *Nevada*'s state trees, the single-leaf pinyon, also has tasty nuts. The main difference between the two trees is that New Mexico's tree has needles that grow in bundles of two or sometimes three rather than singly. Both trees are able to grow in dry, rocky soils, and both have short, stout trunks and straggly branches. The pinyon is usually taller, about 35 feet (10.5 m) tall. The nuts grow under the thick scales of the cones.

The New Mexico Federation of Women's Clubs selected the pinyon, and it was adopted as the state tree in 1949. Every few years the trees produce an extra-good crop of nuts, and people hurry to gather them. In the winter, burning pinyon logs perfume the air of villages and towns throughout the state.

NEW YORK

★ ▬▬▬▬▬ ★

Sugar Maple [*Acer saccharum*]

We may think of the sugar maple as the tree that gives us maple syrup. It is also a beautiful shade tree, and its wood is used to make floors, furniture, and many other everyday things. Most sugar maple trees are 60 to 80 feet (18 to 24 m) tall. The leaves usually have five lobes with a U-shaped division between the lobes. The leaves come out at about the same time as the small, yellowish flowers, which droop from long, slender stems. The fruits have two wings. By midsummer the seeds within ripen and are ready to fly away. By autumn the leaves are masses of golden yellow tinged with scarlet.

In late winter and very early spring, sap begins to flow through the trees. Native Americans taught the early colonists how to get the sap by tapping the trees (making holes in them) and how to boil it down to make syrup. The syrup that we buy today comes from special groves of trees.

New York adopted the sugar maple as its state tree in 1956. The sugar maple is also the state tree of *Vermont*, page 54, *West Virginia*, page 57, and *Wisconsin*, page 58.

NORTH CAROLINA

★ ■■■■■■■■■■ ★

Longleaf Pine [*Pinus palustris*]

In 1963, North Carolina adopted the longleaf pine because it is the most common of all the trees that grow in the state. It is also the most important tree in the history of North Carolina. Its wood and its resin have been used to make many different kinds of products from earliest times to the present. The tree is described under *Alabama*, page 9.

NORTH DAKOTA

★ ■■■■■■■■■ ★

American Elm [*Ulmus americana*]

North Dakota adopted the American elm as its state tree in 1947. Information from the state says it was adopted because it is "a beautiful, spreading shade tree that is common over much of North America. It is a favorite home for many birds, and its wood is used mostly for flooring and furniture." The tree is described under *Massachusetts*, page 30.

OHIO

Ohio Buckeye (or Buckeye) [*Aesculus glabra*]

Native Americans gave Ohio's state tree its name. The shiny brown seeds looked to them like the eyes of a white-tailed buck deer, and they called it a buckeye tree. Buckeye trees are generally 20 to 40 feet (6 to 12 m) tall, but some are much taller. The leaves are made up of leaflets, usually five, that fan out from the top of the leafstalks. The greenish-yellow flowers ripen into leathery capsules with prickly surfaces. Each capsule has one or two seeds. The seeds are not good to eat. The tree is sometimes called the stinking buckeye because its leaves and twigs have a strong smell when crushed. Buckeye trees belong to the horse chestnut family. In 1953 the Ohio buckeye became the official tree of Ohio, and Buckeye became the official nickname of the state and its people.

OKLAHOMA

★ ━━━━━━━ ★

Eastern Redbud [*Cercis canadensis*]

The redbud tree is a beautiful sight when its reddish-pink flowers burst out in early spring. This tree is a member of the legume (pea) family. Its flowers look like pea blossoms, and its seeds grow in pods. It is usually a small tree. The leaves are heart-shaped with smooth edges and pointed tips. The pods are often light rose or brownish rose in color. The name "redbud" comes from the color of the buds that grow on the branches in winter. The tree is sometimes called the Judas tree because it is said that Judas Iscariot, the disciple who betrayed Jesus, hanged himself from a tree of this kind and that the white blossoms turned red with shame. In 1937, Oklahoma adopted the redbud as its state tree because it is beautiful and it grows almost everywhere in the state.

OREGON

Douglas Fir [*Pseudotsuga menziesii*]

Next to the California redwoods, the Douglas fir is the tallest and largest tree in the country. It is not a true fir but a close relative of hemlock trees. It has soft, flat needles that grow all around the branches. The cone of the Douglas fir is unusual because it has bracts (leaflike structures) with long prongs (tongues) that stick out between the scales of the cone. The bark on older trees is thick, red-brown in color, and deeply furrowed. Oregon adopted the Douglas fir in 1939, one year after it became the country's leading timber-producing state, thanks mainly to this very special tree. Many of the tall old trees have been cut down. Many people are trying to save those that remain.

PENNSYLVANIA

★ ━━━━━━━━━━━━━━ ★

Eastern Hemlock [*Tsuga canadensis*]

Pennsylvania adopted the eastern hemlock as its state tree in 1931. The hemlock has a feathery look. Its shiny, flat needles grow on short stalks all around the twigs. But the stalks bend so that the needles seem to be in rows on each side of the twigs, and the twigs look somewhat like feathers. On top of the twigs there is also a row of smaller needles. The small red-brown cones dangle from the tips of the twigs. The trees are often over 80 feet (24 m) tall and are shaped like a pyramid. The bark is rich in tannin, a substance once widely used to tan hides (change hides into leather).

Some people have the idea that the hemlock tree is poisonous. This idea comes from some confusion about the death of the philosopher Socrates, who lived in ancient Greece. Socrates was condemned to die for his teachings. He killed himself by drinking a poisonous brew made from a plant called hemlock. That plant, a member of the parsley family, *is* poisonous. But hemlock trees, members of the pine family, are not.

RHODE ISLAND

★ ▬▬▬▬▬▬ ★

Red Maple [*Acer rubrum*]

In early spring, bright red and orange flowers hang from the bare branches of the red maple tree. They are followed by new leaves that are reddish before they turn green in summer. In autumn the leaves are scarlet. The winged fruits are red, too. Red twigs and buds decorate the tree during the winter. The leaves are similar to sugar maple leaves, but they have deep V-shaped notches between the lobes. The tree is about the same size as the sugar maple. Both are fine shade trees. Older red maples have bark that is dark, ridged, and shaggy. Red maples are often the first trees to take root in wetlands and are common swamp trees, but they also grow on mountain ridges. Rhode Island adopted the red maple, one of its most beautiful woodland trees, in 1964.

SOUTH CAROLINA

★ ━━━━━━━━━━━━━━━━ ★

Cabbage Palmetto (cabbage palm) [*Sabal palmetto*]

The cabbage palmetto became famous in South Carolina's history at the beginning of the Revolutionary War. In a battle fought in 1776, British warships tried to capture Charleston by attacking a fort that the people had built of palmetto logs. But the cannonballs fired by the ships did not destroy the fort. Instead, they sank into the soft, tough logs, and the ships sailed away in defeat. A large cabbage palmetto tree appears on South Carolina's flag. The tree became the state tree in 1939. It is described under *Florida*, page 18.

SOUTH DAKOTA

★ ══════════════ ★

Black Hills Spruce (or white spruce) [*Picea glauca*]

Scientists once thought that the beautiful Black Hills spruce was not a true white spruce. But they have decided that differences between it and other white spruces come from where it grows—in South Dakota's famous Black Hills. This tree grows more slowly than other white spruces. It has more needles on its branches, and they are always bright green to bluish green. The new needles of other white spruces are silvery gray. The cones of the Black Hills spruce are thicker and heavier than other white spruce cones. The champion Black Hills spruce is 96 feet (29 m) tall, although the usual height of this spruce tree is 50 to 75 feet (15 to 23 m). South Dakota's best-known tree became the state tree in 1947.

TENNESSEE

Tulip Tree (or yellow poplar) [*Liriodendron tulipifera*]

Tennessee adopted the tulip tree, or yellow poplar, in 1947 because it grows in every part of the state, and its wood was used to build houses and barns in pioneer days. The tree is described under *Indiana*, page 23.

51

TEXAS

★ ━━━━ ★

Pecan [*Carya illinoensis*]

The pecan tree belongs to the walnut family, and it is a member of the hickory group. It is a tall tree, sometimes 100 feet (30 m) or more, with spreading branches. Each leafstalk has nine to seventeen leaflets. The leaflets have toothed edges and pointed ends. The tiny pistillate flowers are pollinated by staminate flowers that hang down in tassels. The fruit is the pecan nut. The nuts that we buy in stores come from orchards of specially developed trees. Texas adopted the pecan tree in 1919. It is thought that this tree was chosen in memory of a former governor of Texas, James S. Hogg, who died in 1906. He asked that a pecan tree be planted at his grave and that the nuts be given to the people for planting all over the state.

UTAH

Blue Spruce [*Picea pungens*]

Utah adopted the blue spruce as its state tree in 1933. It is one of the most beautiful of all the trees that grow in Utah's mountain forests. The tree is described under *Colorado*, page 14.

VERMONT

★ ▬▬▬▬ ★

Sugar Maple [*Acer saccharum*]

The name "Vermont" makes many people think of maple syrup, perhaps because more maple syrup comes from Vermont than from any other state. Making maple syrup and sugar is called "sug'rin" in Vermont. Sap is collected from the trees in a sugar bush (grove of sugar maple trees) and boiled down in the sugarhouse to make syrup. Vermont adopted the sugar maple in 1949. The tree is described under *New York*, page 41.

VIRGINIA

Flowering Dogwood [*Cornus florida*]

Virginia adopted the flowering dogwood in 1956. It is a native tree that grows almost everywhere in the state, and its flower is the state flower. The tree is described under *Missouri*, page 34.

WASHINGTON

★ ▬▬▬▬▬▬▬▬ ★

Western Hemlock [*Tsuga heterophylla*]

The western hemlock is the tallest of the hemlocks and the one that is most valuable for its wood. Like the eastern hemlock, *Pennsylvania*'s state tree, it is admired for its beauty. It is often twice as tall as its eastern relative, and it has longer needles. On both trees, the needles are dark green and glossy on top. The undersides are a lighter green with two rows of whitish lines down the center. The western hemlock has longer cones, and they do not grow on little stalks. They are attached directly to the branchlets. The bark is a dark reddish brown, and it is scaly and furrowed. In 1947, Washington adopted the western hemlock as its state tree because of its importance as a timber tree.

WEST VIRGINIA

★ ▬▬▬▬▬▬▬▬ ★

Sugar Maple [*Acer saccharum*]

A vote taken among schoolchildren and other groups led to the adoption in 1949 of the sugar maple as West Virginia's state tree. The reasons given by the voters were that it is beautiful and it produces wood for furniture and sap for maple syrup. The tree is described under *New York*, page 41.

WISCONSIN

Sugar Maple [*Acer saccharum*]

Some groups in Wisconsin wanted the white pine to be the state tree. But a vote by the state's schoolchildren chose the sugar maple, and the legislature decided to accept the children's choice. The sugar maple, described under *New York*, page 41, became Wisconsin's state tree in 1949.

WYOMING

★ ▬▬▬▬▬ ★

Plains Cottonwood [*Populus sargentii*]

Wyoming adopted the plains cottonwood in 1947. One special tree growing in Wyoming at that time was said to be the largest cottonwood tree in the world. It was burned up in a wildfire in 1955. A new champion tree was selected to help celebrate Wyoming's 100th birthday in 1990. This tree is in Albany County. It is 64 feet (19.5 m) tall and about 30 feet (9 m) around the trunk. Its branches spread out for more than 100 feet (30 m). The cottonwood tree is described under *Kansas*, page 25.

APPENDIX

State Arbor Days

ALABAMA   last full week in February
ALASKA   third Monday in May
ARIZONA   Friday following April 1 in some counties;
   Friday following February 1 in others
ARKANSAS   third Monday in March
CALIFORNIA   March 7–14
COLORADO   third Friday in April
CONNECTICUT   April 30
DELAWARE   last Friday in April
FLORIDA   third Friday in January
GEORGIA   third Friday in February
HAWAII   first Friday in November
IDAHO   last Friday in April
ILLINOIS   last Friday in April
INDIANA   second Friday in April
IOWA   last Friday in April
KANSAS   last Friday in March
KENTUCKY   first Friday in April
LOUISIANA   third Friday in January
MAINE   third week in May
MARYLAND   first Wednesday in April
MASSACHUSETTS   April 30
MICHIGAN   third week in April
MINNESOTA   last Friday in April
MISSISSIPPI   second Friday in February
MISSOURI   first Friday after the first Tuesday in April
MONTANA   last Friday in April
NEBRASKA   April 22
NEVADA   February 28 in southern Nevada;
   April 23 in northern Nevada
NEW HAMPSHIRE   last Friday in April
NEW JERSEY   last Friday in April
NEW MEXICO   second Friday in March
NEW YORK   last Friday in April
NORTH CAROLINA   first Friday following March 15
NORTH DAKOTA   first Friday in May
OHIO   last Friday in April

OKLAHOMA   Friday following the second Monday
    in February
OREGON   last Friday in April
PENNSYLVANIA   last Friday in April
RHODE ISLAND   last Friday in April
SOUTH CAROLINA   first Friday in December
SOUTH DAKOTA   last Friday in April
TENNESSEE   first Friday in March
TEXAS   third Friday in January
UTAH   third Friday in April
VERMONT   first Friday in May
VIRGINIA   second Friday in March
WASHINGTON   second Wednesday in April
WEST VIRGINIA   second Friday in April
WISCONSIN   last Friday in April
WYOMING   last Monday in April

FOR FURTHER READING

Boulton, Carolyn. *Trees*. Illust. by Colin Newman. New York: Franklin Watts, 1984.

Brockman, C. Frank. *Trees of North America: A Field Guide to the Major Native and Introduced Species North of Mexico*. Rev. ed. Illust. by Rebecca Merrilees. Ed. by Herbert S. Zim. New York: Golden Press, 1986.

Dickinson, Jane. *All About Trees*. Illust. by Anthony D'Adamo. Mahwah, N.J.: Troll Associates, 1983.

Earle, Olive. *State Trees*. New York: William Morrow, 1973 (newly rev.).

Jennings, Terry. *Trees*. Chicago: Childrens Press, 1989.

Langley, Andrew. *Trees*. Rev. ed. New York: Franklin Watts, 1987.

Nelson, Cora. *Trees*. New York: Sterling Publishing, 1990.

Schneider, Bill. *The Tree Giants*. Illust. by D. D. Dowden. Helena, Mont.: Falcon Pr. Publishing, 1988.

Zim, Herbert S., and Martin, Alexander C. *Trees: A Guide to Familiar American Trees*. Rev. ed. Illust. by Dorothea and Sy Barlowe. New York: Golden Press, 1987.

Encyclopedia articles on trees (general) and on individual trees.

INDEX

Alabama, 9

Alaska, 10

American elm
    (Massachusetts, North
    Dakota state tree), 30, 43

American holly (Delaware
    state tree), 17

Arbor Day, 7, 60–61

Arizona, 11

Arkansas, 12

Bald cypress (Louisiana state
    tree), 27

Black Hills spruce (South
    Dakota state tree), 50

Blue spruce (Colorado, Utah
    state tree), 14, 53

Bristlecone pine (Nevada state
    tree), 37

Cabbage palmetto (Florida,
    South Carolina state tree),
    18, 49

California, 13

Ceiba (Puerto Rico tree), 15

Coast redwood (California
    state tree), 13

Colorado, 14

Connecticut, 16

Delaware, 17

Douglas fir (Oregon state
    tree), 46

Earth Day, 7

Eastern cottonwood (Kansas,
    Nebraska state tree), 25, 36

Eastern hemlock
    (Pennsylvania state tree), 47

Eastern redbud (Oklahoma
    state tree), 45

Eastern white pine (Maine,
    Michigan state tree), 28, 31

Florida, 18

Flowering dogwood (Missouri,
    Virginia state tree), 34, 55

Georgia, 19

Hawaii, 20

Idaho, 21

Illinois, 22

Indiana, 23

Iowa, 24

Kansas, 25

Kentucky, 26

Kentucky coffee tree,
    (Kentucky state tree), 26

Kukui (Hawaii state tree), 20

Live oak (Georgia state tree), 19

Longleaf pine (Alabama, North
    Carolina state tree), 9, 42

Louisiana, 27

Maine, 28

Maryland, 29

Massachusetts, 30

Michigan, 31

Minnesota, 32

Mississippi, 33
Missouri, 34
Montana, 35

Nebraska, 36
Nevada, 37
New Hampshire, 38
New Jersey, 39
New Mexico, 40
New York, 41
North Carolina, 42
North Dakota, 43
Northern red oak (New Jersey state tree), 39

Oak (Iowa state tree), 24
Ohio, 44
Ohio buckeye (Ohio state tree), 44
Oklahoma, 45
Oregon, 46

Paloverde (Arizona state tree), 11
Pecan (Texas state tree), 52
Pennsylvania, 47
Pinyon (New Mexico state tree), 40
Plains cottonwood (Wyoming state tree), 59
Ponderosa pine (Montana state tree), 35
Puerto Rico, Commonwealth of, 15

Red maple (Rhode Island state tree), 48
Red pine (Minnesota state tree), 32
Rhode Island, 48

Shortleaf pine (Arkansas state tree), 12
Sierra redwood (California state tree), 13
Single-leaf pinyon (Nevada state tree), 37
Sitka spruce (Alaska state tree), 10
South Carolina, 49
South Dakota, 50
Southern magnolia (Mississippi state tree), 33
State Arbor Days, 60–61
Sugar maple (New York, Vermont, West Virginia, Wisconsin state tree), 41, 54, 57, 58

Tennessee, 51
Texas, 52
Tulip tree (Indiana, Tennessee state tree), 23, 51

Utah, 53

Vermont, 54
Virginia, 55

Washington, 56
Western hemlock (Washington state tree), 56
Western white pine (Idaho state tree), 21
West Virginia, 57
White birch (New Hampshire state tree), 38
White oak (Connecticut, Illinois, Maryland state tree), 16, 22, 29
Wisconsin, 58
Wyoming, 59

ABOUT THE AUTHOR

Sue R. Brandt has lived in six of the fifty states—California, Colorado, Illinois, Michigan, Missouri (born there), and New York. She is a graduate of the University of Chicago, has taught school in Missouri, Illinois, and Michigan, and has worked as an editor in both Chicago and New York. Mrs. Brandt was the editor in charge of articles about the fifty states of the United States for the first edition of *The New Book of Knowledge* and later executive editor of that children's encyclopedia. She was also a member of the editorial staff of the *Encyclopedia Americana*. Mrs. Brandt is the author of three other books published by Franklin Watts: *State Flags, Facts About the 50 States,* and *How to Write a Report.*